Text copyright © 2002 by Phyllis Root

Illustrations copyright © 2002
by James Croft

All rights reserved

First edition 2002

ISBN 0-7636-1361-4

2 4 6 8 10 9 7 5 3

Printed in Hong Kong

This book was typeset in Letraset Arta.
The illustrations were done in
acrylic and pastel.

www.candlewick.com

C P
CANDLEWICK PRESS

Learn more at www.brandnewreaders.com

# BRAND NEW READERS™

# Is it a bird?
# Is it a plane?
# No, it's Super Mouse!

Includes advice to help you guide and
support your brand-new reader.

It's Super Mouse!

Super Mouse jumps off a step.

Super Mouse jumps off a box.

Super Mouse jumps off a rock.

Super Mouse jumps off a fence.

Super Mouse jumps off a hill.

Super Mouse flies!

OOF! Super Mouse lands.

# HELPING YOUR BRAND-NEW READER

**Here's how to make first-time reading easy and fun:**

▶ Read the introduction at the beginning of the book aloud. Look through the pictures together so that your child can see what happens in the story before reading the words.

▶ Read the first page to your child, placing your finger under each word.

▶ Let your child touch the words and read the rest of the story. Give him or her time to figure out each new word.

▶ If your child gets stuck on a word, you might say, *"Try something. Look at the picture. What would make sense?"*

▶ If your child is still stuck, supply the right word. This will allow him or her to continue to read and enjoy the story. You might say, *"Could this word be 'ball'?"*

▶ Always praise your child. Praise what he or she reads correctly, and praise good tries too.

▶ Give your child lots of chances to read the story again and again. The more your child reads, the more confident he or she will become.

▶ Have fun!

CANDLEWICK PRESS
2067 Massachusetts Avenue
Cambridge, MA 02140

Learn more at www.brandnewreaders.com

# Mouse and Dog know
# how to find tasty treats!

Includes advice to help you guide and
support your brand-new reader.

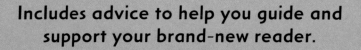

Mouse finds cookies.

Mouse finds apples.

Dog finds a bone.

Mouse and Dog have a picnic.

Mouse finds bread.

Mouse finds cheese.

Mouse finds strawberries.

Mouse finds Dog.

# HELPING YOUR BRAND-NEW READER

## Here's how to make first-time reading easy and fun:

▶ Read the introduction at the beginning of the book aloud. Look through the pictures together so that your child can see what happens in the story before reading the words.

▶ Read the first page to your child, placing your finger under each word.

▶ Let your child touch the words and read the rest of the story. Give him or her time to figure out each new word.

▶ If your child gets stuck on a word, you might say, *"Try something. Look at the picture. What would make sense?"*

▶ If your child is still stuck, supply the right word. This will allow him or her to continue to read and enjoy the story. You might say, *"Could this word be 'ball'?"*

▶ Always praise your child. Praise what he or she reads correctly, and praise good tries too.

▶ Give your child lots of chances to read the story again and again. The more your child reads, the more confident he or she will become.

▶ Have fun!

# Mouse is fast,
# but Cat is faster!

Includes advice to help you guide and
support your brand-new reader.

Learn more at www.brandnewreaders.com

Mouse runs.

Cat runs after Mouse.

Mouse runs under a fence.

Cat runs after Mouse.

Mouse runs up a hill.

Cat runs after Mouse.

Cat tags Mouse.

Mouse runs after Cat.

# HELPING YOUR BRAND-NEW READER

## Here's how to make first-time reading easy and fun:

▶ Read the introduction at the beginning of the book aloud. Look through the pictures together so that your child can see what happens in the story before reading the words.

▶ Read the first page to your child, placing your finger under each word.

▶ Let your child touch the words and read the rest of the story. Give him or her time to figure out each new word.

▶ If your child gets stuck on a word, you might say, *"Try something. Look at the picture. What would make sense?"*

▶ If your child is still stuck, supply the right word. This will allow him or her to continue to read and enjoy the story. You might say, *"Could this word be 'ball'?"*

▶ Always praise your child. Praise what he or she reads correctly, and praise good tries too.

▶ Give your child lots of chances to read the story again and again. The more your child reads, the more confident he or she will become.

▶ Have fun!

**BRAND NEW READERS**™

# When Mouse burns his dinner, he knows just what to do!

**Includes advice to help you guide and support your brand-new reader.**

Mouse makes toast.

The toast burns.

Mouse makes soup.

The soup burns.

Mouse makes peas.

The peas burn.

Mouse makes a phone call.

Pizza!

# HELPING YOUR BRAND-NEW READER

**Here's how to make first-time reading easy and fun:**

▶ Read the introduction at the beginning of the book aloud. Look through the pictures together so that your child can see what happens in the story before reading the words.

▶ Read the first page to your child, placing your finger under each word.

▶ Let your child touch the words and read the rest of the story. Give him or her time to figure out each new word.

▶ If your child gets stuck on a word, you might say, *"Try something. Look at the picture. What would make sense?"*

▶ If your child is still stuck, supply the right word. This will allow him or her to continue to read and enjoy the story. You might say, *"Could this word be 'ball'?"*

▶ Always praise your child. Praise what he or she reads correctly, and praise good tries too.

▶ Give your child lots of chances to read the story again and again. The more your child reads, the more confident he or she will become.

▶ Have fun!